THE SMALLEST

of Things

Robert J. Alves

The Smallest of Things
By Robert J. Alves

Illustrations: Lara Grobler

Book design and layout: Sadie Butterworth-Jones
www.luneviewpublishing.co.uk

Hardback ISBN 979-8-9873646-0-4
eBook ISBN 979-8-9873646-1-1

Lavender (Lavendula)

A young boy with autism struggles to understand and reach out to a confusing and seemingly lonely world. Then, one day he makes a unique friend that will turn his world on end and begin to open his eyes and mind.

His new friend will teach him new ways to interact and communicate, not just with each other, but also in a manner that will strengthen and restore the lost bond with his mother.

Contents

1. Garden Greetings

Ari sat quietly in the garden. This was the one place where Mollie, Ari's mother, could really rely on him relaxing.

The garden was bordered by blackberries, raspberries, and all sorts of fruiting vines. Everything was planted in such a way that it provided seclusion from the hustle and bustle of the noisy world that lay just beyond.

This was Ari's sanctuary, a place that he could see and touch. It gave him a feeling of being connected to something much larger than what he could explain to others. The garden was his escape from some of the limitations that, for whatever reason, found their way into his life at a very young age.

The garden's entrance was a rather large arbor, towering ten feet into the air! Flowering vines grew thick on the entrance and covered every possible inch. These plants provided shade from the afternoon summer sun.

In the center of the garden was a small Japanese maple that would turn orange when the days grew shorter. A shallow pond lay just beyond where brightly colored koi fish would splash about.

The rest of the garden was filled with dozens of blooming flowers, and herbs. Honeybees, bumble bees, and wasps seemed to come from every corner of this small world! They flew darting back and forth nonstop, using every possible flower as a landing zone.

When the wind stirred, the air would be filled with the most wonderful smells. This is where Ari found his peace. His mind could run free, and he could seemingly join in on all the activities found here. And, just like nearly every day when he wasn't in school, this is where Ari found himself.

Mollie sat Ari in his chair, which had huge brightly colored pillows that he could pull in around himself. Tussling his hair, she bent down to kiss his cheek and whispered in his ear, "Do you need anything?"

Ari's shoulders drew up as if his neck was touched by a cold wind. He shook his head slightly to indicate that he was fine, and Mollie dropped her hands from his shoulders and walked slowly back into the house.

Ari now sat alone in his chair, watching everything in the garden. This is how he preferred things; being alone in his thoughts.

His view of the garden was much different from what other people could see. When he was there, everything in the garden was his size. Or was he, everything else's size?

Either way, he sat watching, thinking, and then slowly dozing off to sleep under the arbor in the warmth of the sun.

The sun slowly arched across the sky as he dozed; suddenly, his chair was bumped, and Ari's eyes shot open. His eyes slowly brought the garden back into focus, and he waited for the rest of his body to catch up after having been asleep. Ari nervously looked around the best he could to see what had happened.

After what seemed like several minutes, he heard a voice come from behind him. "Oh, excuse me. I was catching my lunch, and I happened to bump into your chair by accident!"

Ari sat motionless, as this was certainly not Mollie's voice, and he had been the only one in the garden for quite some time. He slowly turned his head, straining with all his might to do so, without moving the rest of his body, almost like he was an owl.

What he saw next, gave him quite a scare! He tried to shrink into his chair and pull the pillows around him like a fort. The voice chuckled a little bit, and its owner slowly moved around to the front of the chair. "You don't need to be afraid of me. I don't harm people." The voice said, softly.

Ari looked out from under his pillows so that he could see a little better. "Wha... wha... what are you?" Ari spoke, a little shaken.

The voice, which now had a complete body, sat down in front of him and said, "I am a jumping spider." The voice then continued, "My name is Gemma Salticidae. But you can call me Gemma. It's much easier to say."

Ari emerged slightly from the pillow fort and looked out at her. She was very pretty. She had huge, dark green eyes that glistened and were attached to a very fury silver and black body. She had two longer wisps of hair on each side of her head like long eyelashes.

After a minute of looking at Gemma, Ari decided that she seemed safe and was not going to hurt him. Cautiously, he took a deep breath and managed to squeak out a reply, "My name is Ari."

Gemma moved in a little closer and then turned around and sat next to Ari so that she could also look out over the garden with him. Gemma was very smart, and she knew that sitting next to Ari allowed him a little more time to get comfortable with her and what she was.

After a bit, Ari spoke up. "How is it that I can hear you, and you can hear me?" he said, feeling a little more comfortable with the new guest.

Gemma tucked her lunch under her arm and leaned over toward him. "There are many humans in the world, Ari," she said. Then she leaned in closer to his side and said, "Some of those are very special people who take time to see us." Then she leaned in even closer and whispered in his ear, "but only a VERY special few can actually hear and talk with us."

Ari had never felt special before, and he smiled at the thought that he could be one of those few. Ari, now feeling braver, leaned in closer to Gemma and whispered back, "I've never had a friend before. Of course, I've never spoken to a spider before, either."

Gemma put her furry paw on Ari's arm and almost in a singing voice said, "Well today is a very special day indeed, then!" She looked at him and brushed the hair out of his eyes so that they could look at each other. "Ari, you not only have spoken to a spider, but you also have made a new friend!" she said while patting his arm.

Ari smiled and sat back in the chair and adjusted the pillows so that Gemma could have a place to sit. Gemma happily jumped up onto the chair, and the two new friends sat quietly together.

2. Dangerous Places

Over the passing days, Gemma and Ari became close friends. Ari loved his time in the garden, especially when Gemma was there! They sat in Ari's oversized chair together, which Mollie would set out each day under the arbor.

One day, the two friends sat quietly buried in pillows watching all the various activities of the garden when Gemma spoke up. "The garden is really a wonderful place. Many things coming and going... Some of which are always in too much of a hurry," she paused for a moment to scowl at a honeybee that was flying way too fast.

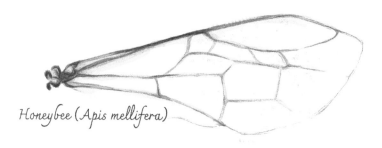

Honeybee (Apis mellifera)

Gemma turned towards Ari and said, "But you MUST be careful!"

Ari picked at a small spot of dirt that had gotten on his hoodie, and then looked up. "Why is that?"

"Some things are just VERY dangerous" Gemma said using one of her legs to point out all the areas in the garden. "Oh, they don't mean to be dangerous, Ari, and they ALL have very important functions in the garden. However, you must always be respectful and be very aware of them."

"What for instance?" Ari said, popping straight up out of the pillows like a gopher and carefully looking around at everything.

"Well," said Gemma glancing around. "Look over there!" She pointed to a web that was in a very low, dark corner of the garden where some pots and tools had been left.

Gemma looked back at Ari and took his face in her furry paws, "That is the home of a black widow. She is VERY poisonous and could make you or your mother quite sick." Gemma's green eyes suddenly reflected an image of Ari and the shocked look on his face.

Ari's eyes grew wide, "W... wh... wh... well, should we get Mollie to kill her?" he said, stammering to get his words out over the thought of this creature being in the garden.

Gemma tapped Ari's forehead to get him to refocus on what she was saying. "Remember this, Ari, ALL of the creatures, right down to the smallest of things in the garden, have a purpose, and they want to live as much as you or me." Gemma continued, "Spiders help keep a balance by preventing various creatures from getting to be too many."

Gemma paused and looked at Ari to make sure he was listening.

"When you get right down to it, we spiders are actually VERY helpful to humans." She sat up proudly and then pointed back at the dangerous area.

"Black widows are just part of that whole process. They, and other spiders, do their job in keeping other insects from getting out of control," Gemma finished speaking and sat quietly.

Ari thought and then questioned, "Well, why does she bite people then?"

"Oh, she doesn't mean to bite people," Gemma said quickly. "Black widows are just skittish, which means they are easily scared, and their reaction can be to bite in order to protect themselves." She then continued, "Most people that get bit, simply did not pay attention to what they touched, what they picked up, or where they were walking."

Gemma thought, paused, then looked back to the web in the corner of the garden.

"Just to be safe, it's best that you try to stay away from that spot and try to let Mollie know that THAT particular spider is there. Make sure you wear your shoes and ALWAYS look before you pick something up."

Gemma tapped Ari again on the forehead with each word she spoke to make sure he fully understood. Ari squirmed and laughed because her paws felt like a soft bristle brush.

"What other sorts of things should we look out for?" questioned Ari, who was now trying to get a closer look around. As much time as he had spent in the garden, he had never considered that there could be dangerous things hidden among all the quiet and seemingly peaceful areas.

Monarch Butterfly (Danaus plexippus)

Gemma stopped poking Ari's forehead and looked around. "OH, perfect example! Look over that at that huge plant with the pink and white flowers." Gemma once again pointed out a location.

Ari turned to Gemma, "You mean the one with all those butterflies on it?"

"Yes, that's the one!" Gemma said as Ari turned his head back to the spot. Gemma jumped down and perched herself on a large stone that was in front of Ari. She then turned around to face him and sat straight up like she was teaching a class.

She cleared her throat and then began to speak like she was a college professor.

"That is called Milkweed." Gemma snapped her leg again in the direction of the plant. "It's very pretty but can also be poisonous," she said, cocking her head to the side to make sure Ari understood.

"Well, then why does Mollie have that plant in the garden?" Ari said, sounding a little irritated. "I mean why have that particular plant if it's poisonous?" He was now practically standing in his chair pointing at the plant.

"Ahh!" said Gemma in a slow warm tone that helped Ari to calm down. "Look at those huge butterflies that are landing on it" once again pointing. "Those are called Monarch butterflies, and people call them important pollinators. Unfortunately, even though humans know how important they are, that particular butterfly is becoming hard to find because their food is being destroyed. Do you know, their baby caterpillars EAT the milkweed plant, which makes THEM poisonous so that birds and other creatures don't, in turn, eat them. Mollie has done a great thing by planting it and giving them a place to live and food to eat."

"Yes!" Exclaimed Gemma. "The garden is truly a wonderful place, and you can learn so much!" She then twirled around to showcase the entire area.

3. Learning and Growing

As the days progressed Gemma taught Ari all about the garden and the creatures that liked to visit and call it home. Another guest that would stop in and say hello from time to time was a great golden wasp, whose name was Dott.

She was beautiful! Her armor was the color of burnt orange like a sunset, and her head was gold as though she wore a crown. Dott had huge black eyes and she flew by using massive wings, the deepest and darkest of blues.

Ari loved all his new friends, but Gemma had become his best friend! On this day he happened to be watching Gemma jumping and moving about the garden.

Great Golden Digger Wasp (Sphex ichneumoneus)

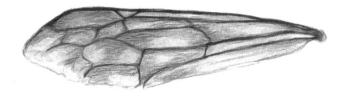

Gemma was very busy working to capture her lunch, and she paused a moment and started to think about her new friend.

Ari wasn't as smelly as other humans, but not quite as clean either. His head had thick dark hairs, but his arms didn't have a single wisp of hair. He wore a baggy set of clothes that he referred to as sweatpants and a hoodie. His hoodie was orange and white and featured some kind of design. He told Gemma that his hoodie represented something called a sports team, but he didn't know exactly what sport they played.

His eyes were bright blue but much too small to see anything of importance. His fangs were small and well hidden in his mouth. *With only two legs, how could he possibly hope to catch his food?* she wondered.

He also seemed rather scrawny for a human. He was shorter and thinner than most of the boys his age. *Perhaps his mother doesn't feed him enough flies and grubs.* She glanced over at him and chuckled.

Gemma continued her assessment, and wondered, *Seriously? No fur tufts, no gripping claws on his hands to hold and climb with! She thought to herself, Honestly, how do these HUMANS survive?*

Accidently speaking out loud, "and, Only TWO eyes!" Gemma shook her head as if shaking off rain drops. "Total silliness" she said while making a jump back towards the chair.

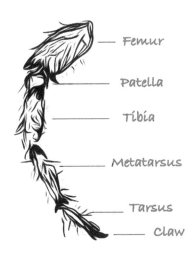

"Yeah, well….," Ari said after overhearing, "you're not all that either!" He smirked and then playfully scowled while sticking out his tongue.

Gemma crawled up and sat on the arm of Ari's chair, and they laughed at each other. Then, while still laughing, she said, "It is great that we can laugh at and with each other!" After a few seconds, Gemma said thoughtfully, "We are connected."

"What do you mean?" Ari said while getting comfortable in the chair.

Gemma placed her paw on his shoulder and then looked out across the garden. "Oh, Ari, don't you know? There are many flowers, trees, and creatures in this world. A good share of them may be the same type of plant or from the same home in the ground. But even then, we are all uniquely made for our purpose. Look at how the wind blows about those flowers. They all look alike. They are all the same plant. But, take a really good look."

Ari squinted at the flowers she was pointing to.

Green darner (Anax junius)

Gemma continued, "The petals on that one are just a bit smaller. OH, and look! Even though the wind blows from the same direction, they ALL move separately. See how they are all moving, not always together, but still connected nonetheless? We do not look like each other, but don't we live and move together, and certainly help each other?"

"I protect you and your food from other insects, and you give me this garden to live in. If you really think about it, Ari, we really are all connected. I think we were friends before we even really knew it."

Gemma paused and reflected. "Yes, caring for and protecting each other."

Ari smiled and tossed his arm across Gemma giving her a hug. They both settled back into the chair to watch their garden.

German chamomile (Matricaria recutita)

4. Overcoming

The next day, Ari's mother Mollie, carried the chair to the garden, dropping a few pillows along the way. She scooted them along with her foot the best she could. Finally arriving at the garden, Mollie arranged the chair, fluffed the pillows, and headed back to the house.

This was almost a daily routine for Mollie during the summer months, unless it was raining and also on the days that Ari just could not attend his school classes. Once back at the house she would then pick up Ari, then carry him outside and get him situated in his spot.

There was just something about the grass that would cause Ari to panic if he had to walk in it. However, once Ari was in the garden and in his chair with his feet off the ground, he would always feel a little more relaxed and not quite so overwhelmed by, well, by everything.

Mollie once again tussled his hair, bent down to kiss his cheek, and asked the daily question, "Do you need anything?" Today, though, was unusual. Instead of just a small shrug, Ari mouthed a word.

An almost imperceptible whisper of a "no" drifted from Ari's lips. She stood still for a moment, not sure if that was what she heard or if it was just the sound of the garden.

She gave him another hug and disappeared back into the house wishing he would wear something else besides a hoodie, especially when it was so warm out. After what seemed like forever, Gemma showed up and sat next to Ari.

"You know, it always seems so loud in the house," Ari said breaking the momentary silence. "So loud at times that Mollie has had to cover my ears! It can make things confusing and hard for me to think."

Gemma sat quietly listening and watching over her friend.

Ari continued, "I don't understand Gemma. I can walk, talk, and play with you. But, when it comes to Mollie and other humans, nothing seems to work right."

Ari looked down at the ground sadly, then over at Gemma.

"I don't see them like I see you, Gemma. My arms don't always seem to work. Sometimes it's hard to control what I actually want them to do. I cannot look anyone in eyes." Ari sat for a moment reflecting on everything.

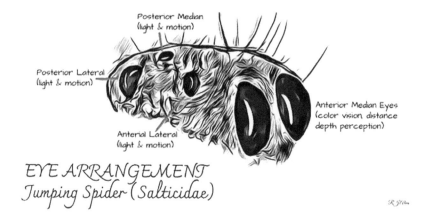

Posterior Median
(light & motion)

Posterior Lateral
(light & motion)

Anterior Median Eyes
(color vision distance
depth perception)

Anterior Lateral
(light & motion)

EYE ARRANGEMENT
Jumping Spider (Salticidae)

Ari now in total frustration, "I can't even speak to them like I do you! If it wasn't for you Gemma, I would have no one to talk to." He slowly lowered his head and focused again on the pond.

Gemma scratched her head and thought. Then, she placed her furry paw on his arm.

"Well, it is true, you can look at and talk with me," Gemma said. "Maybe you can just try to pretend that Mollie looks like me?"

"OH! I do LOVE your eyes, Gemma!" Ari perked up and excitedly turned to face her.

"Do you know I can see better than some humans?" Gemma said proudly. "I can see where I have gone before I even get there. I can even see in colors that humans can't!" she continued to gloat.

Ari snorted, "I can see in all sorts of colors too!" He then got quiet, looked down, and spoke almost in a whisper, "Sometimes though, the colors can be a little jumbled."

"ALRIGHT!" Gemma quickly shouted to get him to cheer up. "Tonight, when Mollie catches your food, pretend that she looks like me!"

Ari thought, looked at the pond for several minutes, and then thought some more.

"That's a GREAT idea!" Ari trumpeted, startling Gemma out of the chair. "When I go back in for food, I will pretend that Mollie looks like you!" He beamed with delight.

Gemma picked herself off the ground and chuckled imagining a spider walking around in human clothes. She said, "Once you get the hang of that, Ari, I can then maybe help you work on the other things you have problems with."

"You have some great ideas, and I sure thank you for helping me," Ari said, and without thinking reached over to pick grass off her face.

5. It's What's for Lunch

Ari and Gemma returned to sitting quietly in the garden, both still looking out over the pond counting the ripples created by leftover raindrops that were falling from the leaves of the tree. Ari drew his feet a little tighter in to the chair and breathed slow and deep.

He then pulled the pillows in a little closer but made sure that Gemma had plenty of room and that she was just as comfortable. "What does that taste like?" Ari said looking over to Gemma, who was silently munching on a big, fat, juicy, fly.

Gemma stopped chewing, wiped her mouth, and looked thoughtfully at him. "I've never had human food before, Ari."

She thought a little longer trying to think of what she could compare her lunch to.

Looking at Ari and taking another mouthful of food she mumbled, "Hmm, I've only seen these and never tried them, but I would say that they are like raisins?"

They both turned their attention back to the pond. "Do you like raisins?" Gemma asked, once again breaking the silence.

"I don't think I have ever tried one before," Ari responded. "There is something about some food that just doesn't feel right. Mollie always makes me some kind of food out of chicken that she calls nuggets." Ari continued, "That seems to be the only thing that I like to eat. Everything else is just weird."

Gemma now sat thinking.

"Well, what do these chicken nuggets taste like?" Gemma asked curiously.

Ari smiled, turning to her and said, "I've never had spider food before, so I would say they are like caterpillars."

Taking another mouthful of her lunch Gemma enthusiastically replied "OH! That sounds absolutely fantastic, Ari!"

They both then turned their attention back to the pond. About this time Dott flew in, sounding like the engines of a jumbo jet! Settling in next to Ari and Gemma, Dott looked out over the garden with them.

Mountain Mint (Pycnanthemum muticum)

"What's the conversation?" Dott said while stroking her long antenna.

"We are talking about what's for lunch," Ari said without even looking over to Dott. He then continued, "What do you like to eat?"

Dott let go of her antenna and it made a *thwhip* sound and looked over at the flowers and pointed "THAT is my favorite!"

Ari sat puzzled, "As big and tough as you are, I thought you ate other insects."

Dott laughed "HA! You and all humans seem to think the same thing! Just because I look mean and very impressive," Dott spoke while standing up and stretching out her wings. "Don't just assume you know what I eat or that I'm mean," she said, now doing a perfect twirl like a ballet dancer.

"I would rather not get into fights; they are a waste of energy. If people would stop swatting at me. Or, if they would stop screeching and screaming like a beetle-brain when I fly by, they certainly wouldn't get stung!"

Green June Beetle (Cotinis nitida)

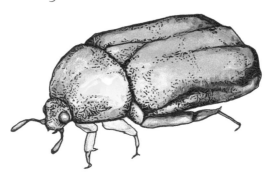

Dott then turned to Ari. "Without me, the bees, and other wasps, there would be no flowers OR food for humans. We are the pollinator crew," she said as she flexed four of her legs like a weightlifter. "And, do you know my favorite thing is the sweet, sugary, nectar from flowers!"

"Nectar?" Ari said, now examining the flowers the best he could from the chair.

"Yes, nectar" Dott said politely. "I think you would call it juice" she turned to look at him and laughed.

"I do LOVE juice! I can only imagine what nectar must be like," Ari said.

Dott then looked out at the garden "Gemma, Ari, please excuse me. I must be leaving as there is much to get done!" She spread her huge wings and darted off as quickly as she arrived, leaving the two friends sitting in the chair looking out over everything.

Feverfew (Tanacetum parthenium)

Holy Basil (Ocimum tenuiflorum)

6. Learning to Hunt

Ari suddenly looked up in thought and blurted out, "will you teach me how to capture my own food?"

Gemma thought, chuckled, and thought again. "Ok, that really is an important thing to know how to do. But first, you need to learn how to see properly." She got up from the chair and walked around Ari as if stalking him like a lion.

"Now, when you find the food you want," Gemma crouched down low, "you have to see it, but act like you don't want it. Just act cool and casual." Gemma walked lazily around him and flipped a leg in the air as if to say hello.

"Ok, got it," Ari said, leaning forward in the chair so that he could watch and listen more closely.

Gemma continued to circle, then came to a complete stop and remained motionless like a stone. "Now, you focus solely on the food, crouch your abdomen back just a b...."

"Abdomen?" Ari blurted out. Gemma paused looking a little irritated.

"Do not interrupt and pay attention," Gemma grumbled, tapping Ari's forehead with her furry paw. "Um, an abdomen, well, for you let's just call it your rear end," Gemma said, breathing deeply and shaking her head. "Stay focused. Crouch your rear end just a bit. Then raise your front arms out just a little, so that you will be able to snatch your food," she said, demonstrating as she spoke.

"Like this?" Ari asked, getting up from his chair and hopping into the grass. Crouching low, he lowered his rear end nearly level with his knees and raised his arms outwardly.

"YES!" Gemma shouted excitedly. She continued her coaching session, "But try not to wobble so much." She silently chuckled in her head at Ari's practicing and thought, *Wobbling wouldn't be an issue if he had more than two legs!*

Gemma chuckled again. "Now, with one big jump, leap at your food and grab it with your front arms!"

Southern Toad (*Anaxyrus terrestris*)

Little did Gemma and Ari know, but Mollie was watching from the kitchen window with great interest. Mollie thought to herself, *Ari never wanted to get out of his chair much less allow his feet to touch the grass!*

Ari crouched and practiced leaping, while Gemma critiqued each effort, swatting his rear end on several attempts. "Keep LOW!" Gemma growled.

After what seemed like several hours, Gemma spoke up "I think you are about ready, Ari."

Ari stopped mid-leap, "Well that's a good thing. Mollie will be coming to take me inside for dinner soon."

Mormon Apricot (Prunus armeniaca)

Early Elberta Peach (Prunus persica)

7. Dinner is Served

No sooner had Ari spoken, than the door opened, and Mollie began to walk into the garden. As Mollie approached, Gemma took a good look at her.

Mollie had reddish hair with tiny specs of red on her nose and cheeks. She had blue eyes, but they were a bit darker than Ari's. She wore a long green colored summer cloth with white dots.

"Quick, Gemma, get in my hoodie!" Ari said, breaking her stare. "I will take you to dinner with me, and you can watch my first capture."

Gemma jumped and seemingly disappeared into Ari's hoodie just in time! Mollie bent down to Ari to pick him up as she always did, but instead, he reached out and took hold of Mollie's hand and slowly started to walk back to the house leading her through the garden while making sure that Gemma was well hidden.

Ari's dinner was typical, the same as every night. Mollie delivered a plate of chicken nuggets and a glass of juice. Gemma moved about to get a better view and watched curiously from her hiding place in the folds of Ari's hoodie.

After a while, Gemma started to grow a little impatient and finally whispered to Ari, "Well, let's get on with this!"

Ari shifted uncomfortably and tugged on his clothes. He then dropped a nugget that he had been eating and looked over to Mollie. Gemma suddenly poked him for a little more encouragement.

"R... Ra... Raisins" Ari struggled to get the word out.

Ari looked up and he remembered his garden training and pretended that Mollie looked like Gemma. He tried hard to focus, and suddenly Mollie resembled Gemma in a green and white polka-dotted summer dress! He was only barely able to keep from laughing out loud.

Mollie suddenly dropped her spoonful of peas and stared at him in shock! She was looking at him, face-to-face, his blue eyes looking into hers, an interaction that the two had not shared in over five years!

Mollie rose as calmly as possible, trying hard to mask her excitement at this new interaction with him. She then went to the cupboard to prepare his new food request. She turned her back to the table and took a bowl out of the cupboard and filled it with a box of raisins. Then she took several slow deep breaths as she fought back tears.

"This is it!" Gemma excitedly whispered. "Get ready!"

Ari crouched in his chair, assuming the position he had practiced all day, and raised his arms outward. He then opened his eyes as large as he possibly could, fixed his gaze on Mollie's back, and waited.

Mollie, by now, had composed her emotions, so she turned around and was startled to notice Ari's unusual sitting position.

Ari's eyes lowered and became focused on the bowl of food. Remembering Gemma's training, he casually turned his head slightly away as if uninterested. Ari thought to himself, *Want it but act like you don't want it.*

Mollie approached the table and was now within four feet of a crouching Ari and hidden Gemma.

"NOW!" Shrieked Gemma, giving him a little pinch.

Ari scooted his rear end backwards, jumped with all his might, and latched onto the bowl with his outstretched hands. The chicken nuggets scattered into the air, and the juice splashed onto the floor. But, Ari was able to clear most of the other dishes. With the skill of an athlete, Ari landed in the middle of the table face down in the bowl of raisins.

"Ole!" Squealed Gemma in approval.

Gemma was so proud and excited for her student, that she leapt from Ari's hoodie and crawled out onto the table.

Mollie was startled at first and let out a small scream of shock at his attack, but then started laughing when Ari looked up with a mouthful of raisins. Mollie happened to look down at the table and froze when she saw the small spider on the dining table. She grabbed a cloth and began to swat at it.

Gemma noticed Mollie swinging a cloth at her. She panicked and tried to scurry to safety but could not find a hiding spot. Suddenly, Gemma felt herself being scooped up by hands she knew!

"GEMMA!" Ari shouted very loudly at Mollie.

Mollie froze, dropped the cloth, and looked at Ari in shock. He slowly raised his cupped hands and opened them so that Mollie could see. Softly he said to her "Gemma," and then he smiled the best he could.

Gemma looked back and forth at Ari and Mollie, then raised her front legs as if in greetings.

Mollie then started to remember Ari's unusual exercises in the garden from earlier and what had just happened, and she finally started to understand. Mollie cupped Ari's hands gently in her own and looked down at the small spider. She then smiled at them both and softly said, "Gemma."

Stinging Nettle (Urtica dioica)

8. That's What Friends Do

The next day, Ari and Gemma sat in the garden, watching, relaxing, and enjoying each other's company. "Thank you, Ari," Gemma said softly as she reflected on the dinner events and what could have happened.

Gemma turned back to look at the pond and then looked up at him. "Gemma, you are my best friend," he said. "You taught me, that no matter how big you are, how tall you are, or how small you are, you can make a difference in someone or something's life."

Ari paused thinking then gave her a hug and said, "Even the smallest of things can make the biggest of changes. Without you, Gemma, I might not have ever been able to talk to my mother!"

Gemma thought about what he said and settled into the chair with Ari. "You know, Ari, you had an easy dinner," she said smugly.

"How so?" Ari responded a little surprised.

Gemma looked at him, "Mollie had obviously peeled your food! I find wings overrated, and they get stuck in your teeth!" she began to snicker.

Ari leaned in giving Gemma another hug. The two friends then returned to staring at the koi pond all the harder.

"Ari?" Gemma spoke after several minutes of concentration.

"Yes Gemma?" he said, not breaking his intense stare from the pond.

Apache Blackberry (Rubus fruticosus)

Gemma turned curiously towards Ari, "We have been staring at this pond for ages. What are we looking for?"

Ari's expression began to change, as one eyebrow raised, and then the other.

Slowly Ari turned to Gemma, his head tilted to one side as if he could not believe the question. "Uhhh" Ari began to say, his mouth now fully open in surprise, "I've been trying to figure out what you were looking at!"

Gemma turned back to the pond as did Ari, in complete silence. Glancing back at each other, small chuckles began to emerge from the two unlikeliest of friends, eventually giving way to full-on laughter.

Gemma jumped and tackled Ari, tickling him with her furry paws, as they both fell into the pond, laughing and scattering koi in a colorful tidal wave of fish.

From the kitchen window, Mollie watched, smiled, and laughed, thankful for her new friend Gemma, and for the smallest of things.

Passion Flower (Passiflora incarnata)

About the Author

My mother understood the importance of starting a child early with reading. I remember her reading the original *Pinocchio* by Carlo Collodi to me. Things do NOT go well with Honest John or Jiminy Cricket! She also read *Alice in Wonderland*, *Charlotte's Web*, and the stories of the Brothers Grimm. Then, when I was old enough to read more advanced books on my own, she bought me the condensed versions of *Oliver Twist*, *The Count of Monte Christo*, and various other works.

In my teens, I loved reading *Tom Sawyer*, short stories by O'Henry, Steinbeck, Edgar Allen Poe, and tall tales by other various authors. My mother taught me that creativity and imagination were undoubtedly just as important as my analytical side. It's one thing to work in a factory turning knobs and dials. It's another to work in a factory turning knobs and dials that create the most wonderful chocolates you could ever imagine! Treat each day as a new adventure, not just a job.

I grew up as a "military brat." My father was a 30-year Air Force veteran, and we sometimes had to be packed and ready to move again at a moment's notice. I have lived primarily in North Carolina since 1982, with the exception of my time being deployed due to my service in the United States Marine Corps.

I have always had a great imagination, with short stories randomly coming to mind. Finally, my wife told me I had to write one of them down. This is how *The Smallest of Things* was born.

My wife, Kelly, has been my "subject matter expert" regarding Ari and how he interacts with the world around him. She has a Doctor of Education degree in curriculum and instruction, specializing in autism education. She also has master's degrees in special education and developmental psychology.

Kelly worked for several years as the director of a K-12 private school for children with autism. I listened to her talk about the students and parents and saw how she interacted with them. I also volunteered several times and was able to work with the students myself.

A few years ago, Kelly and I discovered a love of gardening; of course, not just any gardening, however. We began planting various plants that were beneficial not only to our own health but also to our little friends that often go unnoticed. With this book, I wanted to present something like a beginner expedition guide with simple illustrations that would hopefully spur the reader's imagination. Think of the Lewis and Clark expedition notes where the flowers or various insects were just drawn in the footnotes of the pages.

Through my gardening expeditions, I discovered that I loved interacting with the smallest of things. These adventures have included everything from petting small jumping spiders and rescuing trapped dragonflies to feeding bees a bit of sugar water or honey from the palm of my hand.

I hope that this book will help you to open your eyes and mind to the little things that are all around us. These little things can really make a big difference in your life and open paths of communication with each other.

Compassion for even the smallest of things costs you nothing, but the rewards are priceless.

Wild Bergamot (Monarda fistula)

About the Illustrator

Lara Grobler, raised on a remote farm in the Kammanassie Mountains in South Africa. She and her siblings were homeschooled and allowed every opportunity to paint and illustrate throughout her upbringing. She continued to develop her art, working with gouache paints to create detailed paintings.

Lara now lives with her husband in a little town called Twee Riviere, on a small food forest farm, South Africa. Lara is soon to be a mother and looks forward to the upcoming challenge of caring for their child and managing her illustration work.

Lightning Source UK Ltd.
Milton Keynes UK
UKHW020637160223
417065UK00002B/24

9 798987 364604